MW00934276

Eat Rutabagas

By Jerry Apps

Illustrated By Annika Beatty-Andersen

First Edition

ISBN# 1-930596-08-1

Published by
The Guest Cottage, Inc.
P.O. Box 848
Woodruff, WI 54568
1-800-333-8122

Please write or call for a free catalog of other publications by The Guest Cottage.

Illustrations and Cover Art by Annika Beatty-Andersen
Design by Debra Adams

Printed in the United States of America

Library of Congress Cataloging-in-Publication Data

Apps, Jerold W., 1934-
Eat rutabagas / by Jerry Apps ; illustrations by Annika Beatty-Andersen.
p. cm.
Summary: A farmer is convinced that everyone will love rutabagas as much as he does if only they're grown right, and so he recruits his sons to help prepare the soil and plant, harvest, and sell the crop.
ISBN 1-930596-08-1
[1. Rutabaga--Fiction. 2. Agriculture--Fiction.] I. Beatty-Andersen, Annika, ill. II. Title.
PZ7.A6534 Eat 2002
[Fic]--dc21

2002002439

Dedication

For my grandchildren, Josh, Ben, Christian and Nicholas.

Acknowledgements

Those who helped most with this project were my wife, Ruth, my daughter, Susan Apps Horman and my trusty young consultants, Ben and Josh Horman.

This book is based on a true story.

Pa liked rutabagas.

Ma ate them, but never said she liked them.

My brothers and I didn't like them, but we ate them.

We ate rutabagas in soup and with sauerkraut; we ate them with pork hocks or prepared alone. Pa believed that if everyone had the opportunity to eat good rutabagas, they would like them.

Nobody got around to telling him that just wasn't so.

Ma grew a few rutabagas in the garden, but Pa was never pleased with them, said they weren't right.

"What beggies need"--he called them beggies--"is breaking ground, not soil that's been worked every year."

Breaking ground is soil that has never been plowed.

Pa had his eye on a three-acre patch
of ground on the north edge of our woodlot.
Slowly, over the years, we had cut trees
from this land until now
there were great open areas
between the stumps and remaining trees.
One day, as we cut down
one of the few trees in the area for firewood,
Pa said, "This land will grow beggies."
"Yup, beggies would grow good here. All we gotta do is break this ground and work it up."

The next spring, we began removing
stumps with a little red tractor.
Pa had borrowed a breaking plow from a
neighbor, a single bottom plow that would
cut through tree roots like they were spaghetti.

We hitched the plow to the tractor, which I drove while Pa hung onto the plow handles.
We lunged across the field, slicing through roots, smashing into hidden rocks, and turning over the beautiful virgin soil that had never before been plowed.

At the hardware store, Pa said,
"I want enough beggie seed for
three acres. Got breaking ground
that's good for beggies."

The surprised hardware store clerk said, " You've bought all my rutabaga seed. I'll have none for my other customers."

The only way Pa could figure out how to plant the rutabaga seeds was to sow them by hand.

One spring day, I hiked with him to the breaking ground and he walked back and forth across the new field, flinging the seeds from side to side.

He then covered them with the drag pulled by the little red tractor.

A couple nights later, a gentle, drippy rain began, the kind that occasionally fell in late May. The new field was properly soaked but not drenched.

A week later, when Pa and I were walking the new ground, we saw the first little rutabaga plants beginning to push through the soft, sandy soil.

"Yup, they're coming up," Pa said. "Planted the field just right. Rain couldn't have come better. If the weather is good to us, we're gonna have beggies, lots of beggies."

By late August, purplish-green rutabaga leaves
nearly covered the ground.

The entire three acres was a sea
of waving,
moving
rutabaga plants
foretelling a plentiful harvest of this wonderful
but scarce crop.

Finally it was October and Pa said one day at breakfast, "Let's dig that patch of beggies and see what we got."

Pa and I each shouldered a six-tine barn fork and walked the path through the woods to the beggie patch.

We forked out rutabagas as we would fork out potatoes, except the rutabagas weren't in rows, they were everywhere.

It was a beautiful sight--firm, round, purple and yellowish-white roots popping out of the ground with each stroke of the fork. Rutabaga roots carpeted the ground. There were hundreds of them, thousands of them.

Some were as large as muskmelons; others were as small as onions. A few were long and thin, some were fat and squatty. Each was without blemish, and each was unique but also like every other one.

When we finished the barn chores the next morning, we hitched the little red tractor to the farm wagon and headed for the rutabaga patch. All day, my brothers, Pa and I filled wooden bushel boxes with rutabagas and hauled them to the cellar under the house.

Pa kept count and at the end of the day proudly announced, "We've got three hundred and fifty-two bushels of the best rutabagas you'll find anywhere in the country."

"How we gonna sell all these rutabagas?" I asked. Pa had never talked much about selling the crop, only about growing it.

"Easy," Pa said. "We're gonna peddle them. We'll peddle them from house to house. Sell them one bushel at a time. No time at all and we'll be out of rutabagas and wishing we had grown more. Just wait and see."

The following Saturday, we took the back seat out of our old black car and piled it full of rutabagas. Pa gave us a quick lesson in selling. "Here's how you do it," he said. "You take a good-sized beggie, one that is perfect in every way. You walk up to a house and you knock on the door. When someone comes to the door, you say, "We've got breaking-ground rutabagas for sale. How many bushels would you like? We're selling them for $1.50 a bushel."

On a back street in a small town
not far away, we stopped the old
black car in front of a little white
house with green trim around the
windows. It was a beautiful autumn
day; the tree leaves had turned to
many shades of yellow, red, and brown.
I picked out a perfect rutabaga and
with my brothers walked up to the
door and knocked.

A gray-haired woman answered the door.

"What cute kids! What can I do for you?"

"See this?" I nervously asked as I thrust the rutabaga out so she could see it better.

"Yes."

"We're selling these and they are perfect in every way because we grew them on breaking ground and Pa says people have been waiting to buy rutabagas like these because there just aren't any like them and how many would you like?" I was out of breath when I finished my sales spiel.

"That's quite a lingo you got there, young man." The woman was laughing.

"I've been practicing," I said. "How many would you like?"

"How can I say no? I'll take one."

We ran back to the car where Pa was waiting.
"Sold a bushel, sold a bushel," I said excitedly.
We lifted a heaping bushel of rutabagas from the car. My brothers carried one side and I the other.

We stopped at the bottom of the steps where the gray-haired woman was waiting. She had a quizzical look on her face.
"Where are you going with all those rutabagas?" she asked.
"You said you wanted a bushel. Here it is," I answered with a smile.
"My goodness. My goodness. I wanted one rutabaga, not a whole bushel. How much do you want for one rutabaga?" She picked out a medium-sized one, not even the biggest one in the box.
"I don't know," I stammered. "But I'll find out."

I ran back to the car and asked Pa what we should charge for one rutabaga.

"One rutabaga. She only wants one. Thought she wanted a bushel."

"So did I," I said.

"Charge her a nickel."

And that's how the afternoon went. A nickel here, a nickel there. Once in awhile a dime for two rutabagas. Even one sale of a quarter for five. Not one person--not one--bought an entire bushel, so the old black car was still half full of rutabagas when we returned home.

"Off day," Pa said. "People have forgotten how good beggies can be, especially breaking-ground beggies."

The next Saturday was an off day, too. So was the following week and the week after that. By the time the snow began to fall and the peddling season closed, we hadn't sold twenty bushels of rutabagas. But Pa was ever optimistic.

"We'll sell them in the spring," he said.

In late March, I noticed a strange smell in the house when I came home from school one day. A few days later, Uncle Wilbur stopped by. He no more than got into the house when he said, "There's something spoiled in here." The huge pile of rutabagas had begun to rot, and they sent out a stench like one nobody had ever smelled before. It was worse than strong onions, even worse than rotten eggs.

The following Saturday we hauled baskets of rotten rutabagas up the cellar steps and dumped them into the manure spreader. Pa hauled loads of spoiled rutabagas back to the rutabaga patch where he spread them.
"It's only fitting that they go back where they came from," Pa said.

That spring we planted the breaking ground to oats, and a finer crop of oats we'd never seen.

"At least the oats seem to like the rutabagas," Pa said.